ULTIMATE
FIELD TRIP 4

A WEEK IN THE 1800s

by Susan E. Goodman   photographs by Michael J. Doolittle

ATHENEUM BOOKS FOR YOUNG READERS

To Zach—my New Jersey muse
and to Kayla Ouellette and her bear Oatmeal

—S. G.

To Susan, a great collaborator
and friend

—M. D.

Atheneum Books for Young Readers
An imprint of Simon & Schuster Children's Publishing Division
1230 Avenue of the Americas
New York, New York 10020

Text copyright © 2000 by Susan E. Goodman
Photographs copyright © 2000 by Michael J. Doolittle

Book design by Anne Scatto/PIXEL PRESS
The text of this book is set in Monotype Fournier.
Printed in Hong Kong

10 9 8 7 6 5 4 3 2 1

Library of Congress Cataloging-in-Publication Data
Goodman, Susan E., 1952-
Ultimate Field Trip 4 : A Week in the 1800s / by Susan E. Goodman;
photographs by Michael J. Doolittle.—1st ed. p. cm. Includes bibliographical references.
Summary: Describes the experience of a group of middle school students who spend a week at
Kings Landing Historical Settlement, learning what life was like for young people in the
nineteenth century. ISBN 0-689-83045-9
1. United States—Social life and customs—19th century—Juvenile literature.
2. Children—United States—Social life and customs—19th century—Juvenile
literature. 3. Canada—Social life and customs—19th century—Juvenile literature.
4. Children—Canada—Social life and customs—19th century—Juvenile
literature. 5. Kings Landing Historical Settlement—Juvenile literature. [1. Canada—
Social life and customs—19th century. 2. United States—Social life and customs—
19th century. 3. Kings Landing Historical Settlement. 4. School field trips.]
I. Doolittle, Michael J., ill. II. Title. E337.5.G66 2000 973.5—dc21 99-19156

FIRST
F
EDITION

Acknowledgments

The people at Kings Landing Historical Settlement couldn't have been nicer. Thanks to Bob Dallison for opening his museum to us, Lynn Thornton for paving the way, and all the staff from Norma Reeves, Rebecca Roberts, and Mark Duplisea to Darlene Skidd, Sharlene McEwing, Wendy Coffin, and Susan Hayward, who put up with us and answered our questions. Dawna Gordon graciously put aside a morning to dress a mannequin for us. And a special thanks to all the kids who generously made us a part of their group.

Thanks to readers Deborah Hirschland, Liza Ketchum, Lisa Jahn-Clough, Janet Coleman, and Marjorie Waters for all their insights; Don Heiny and Pete Hvizdak for their help with the photo edit; and to Darrell Butler of Kings Landing for his painstaking expert review of the manuscript.

At Atheneum, we appreciate Caitlin Van Dusen for all her help and patience and Anne Scatto for another beautiful layout. And, Marcia Marshall, thanks yet again for your unending support and encouragement.

Contents

Our group of time travelers (from left to right):
Kneeling: Max Heffler, Megan Stratton, Krista Firlotte, Sarah Glenn, Amy Mollegaard.
Standing: Robin Campbell, Julie Meyer, Holly Cameron, Samantha McIntosh, Jillian Caldwell, Garrett Hockenberry. In the truck: Alex Makkreel, Allison Duffy, Lorena Sivitilli, Stephanie McCracken, Hilary Graham, Erika Mollegaard, Catherine Rousseau, Amanda Scott, Brandon Timberlake, Brandon Moore.

Our group transported to the nineteenth century.

A LEAP BACK IN TIME

IMAGINE TRAVELING back in time to the 1800s. Suddenly, you're in a world without airplanes—or even automobiles. In a hurry to get somewhere? Your best bet, a coach with a team of fresh horses, will zip you along at the breakneck speed of nine miles an hour.

Hungry, but late for school? Forget about popping some instant oatmeal into the microwave. In the 1800s, almost all the foods you eat are made from scratch. If you have toast in the morning, it's because someone in your home has baked the bread and churned the butter that goes with it.

Your nineteenth-century evenings are lit by candles and oil lamps. In a time without telephones, you can talk to friends only when you actually see them. Long-distance communication is by letter—if you know how to write and can afford the postage.

Your music comes from singing and perhaps a friend's fiddle, not radios, tapes, or CDs.

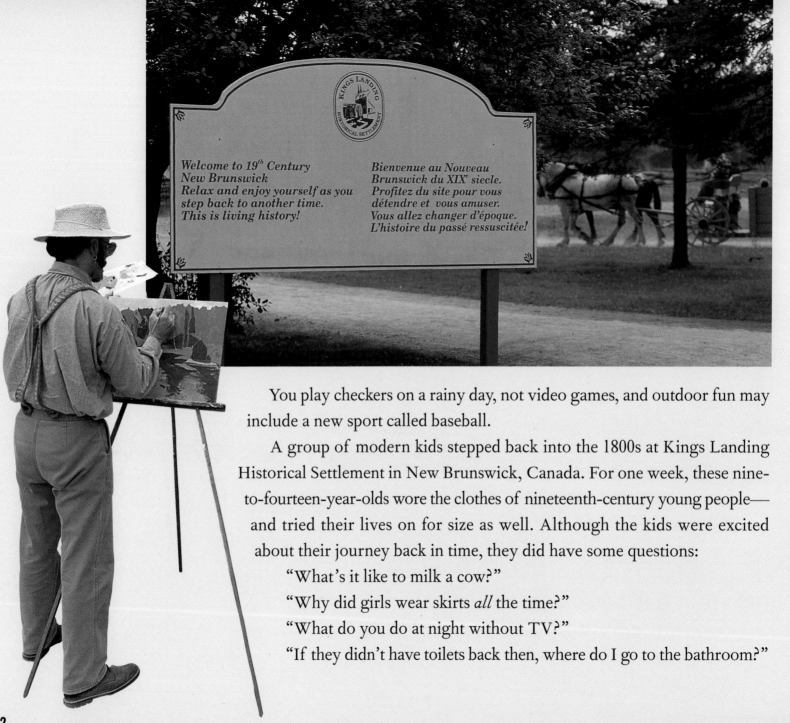

Welcome to 19th Century
New Brunswick
Relax and enjoy yourself as you
step back to another time.
This is living history!

Bienvenue au Nouveau
Brunswick du XIXe siecle.
Profitez du site pour vous
détendre et vous amuser.
Vous allez changer d'époque.
L'histoire du passé ressuscitée!

KINGS LANDING
HISTORICAL SETTLEMENT

You play checkers on a rainy day, not video games, and outdoor fun may include a new sport called baseball.

A group of modern kids stepped back into the 1800s at Kings Landing Historical Settlement in New Brunswick, Canada. For one week, these nine-to-fourteen-year-olds wore the clothes of nineteenth-century young people—and tried their lives on for size as well. Although the kids were excited about their journey back in time, they did have some questions:

"What's it like to milk a cow?"

"Why did girls wear skirts *all* the time?"

"What do you do at night without TV?"

"If they didn't have toilets back then, where do I go to the bathroom?"

STARTING THE JOURNEY

GARRETT HOCKENBERRY sat down with Rebecca, a counselor at Kings Landing.

"Garrett, this week you are going to be a cousin visiting the Heustis household," said Rebecca, introducing him to his nineteenth-century identity. "Your name will be Garrett Heustis."

"That's cool," said Garrett.

"It is," agreed Rebecca, "but since you're going to be living in the nineteenth century this week, 'cool' is one word you shouldn't use. Not 'cool' or 'okay' or 'wow,' because they didn't use those expressions back then. If you

Before entering Kings Landing, the kids got rid of all traces of the twentieth century (except for their braces!).

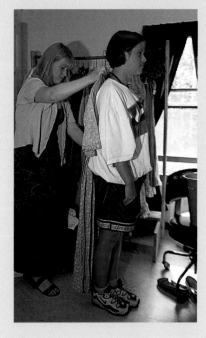

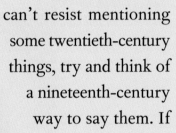

can't resist mentioning some twentieth-century things, try and think of a nineteenth-century way to say them. If you want to talk about your car, for example, you could change the word and say 'wagon.'"

"So . . . my father fixes and sells 'wagons'?" said Garrett, getting into the nineteenth-century spirit of things.

"You've got it!" said Rebecca.

Meanwhile, Norma, the teacher at Kings Landing, was preparing another time traveler. "Did you pack anything modern in your suitcase?" she asked. "Magazines, cameras, earrings, or nail polish?"

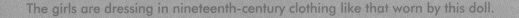
The girls are dressing in nineteenth-century clothing like that worn by this doll.

"No," said Allison, "but I do have some money."

"Money! Young girls from the nineteenth century weren't allowed to carry money," replied Norma. "Give it to your mom to hold for you and you'll be ready to go back in time."

In just moments, Garrett, Allison, and the rest of the group would start their journey. Kings Landing is a special kind of museum, a village of nineteenth-century farms, homes, shops, and mills that bring history to life. All the people who work there dress and act as if they were living in the 1800s. And that's what the kids were going to do as well.

But first they needed to look the part. Those shorts, sneakers, and T-shirts had to go. Next stop— the costume room.

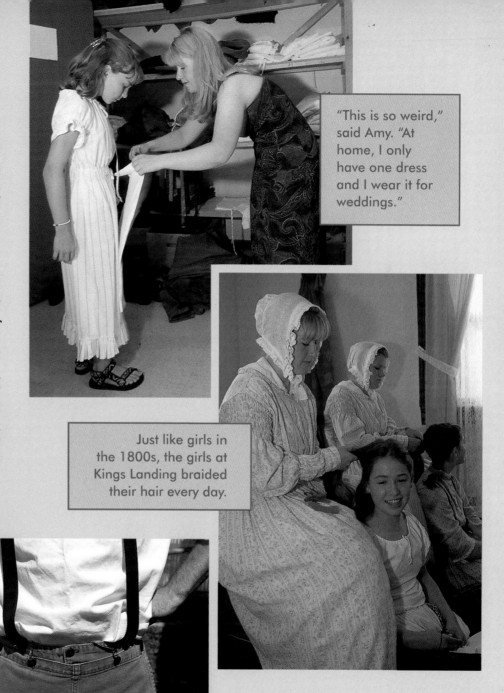

"This is so weird," said Amy. "At home, I only have one dress and I wear it for weddings."

Just like girls in the 1800s, the girls at Kings Landing braided their hair every day.

"I like the shirt and pants," said Max, "but these itchy wool suspenders have got to go."

5

WHAT IS THIS THING?

ANSWER: This iron was heated up by dropping hot wood coals down its spout.

WHAT IS THIS THING?

ANSWER: These ice skates were used by screwing them into your shoes.

"Here's your dress and an apron to keep it clean," said Darlene, the counselor helping the kids with their new outfits. She handed Krista several pieces of clothing.

"What do I do with this one?" Krista asked.

"That's a petticoat; it's like a slip," said Darlene.

"I've never even worn a slip before," said Krista. "What do I do with it?"

Darlene showed Krista how to put her petticoat on underneath her dress, and her apron over it. Then Krista rushed to the mirror. "Wow, this looks really strange, but I guess I'll get used to it."

Most of the kids felt the same way about their new clothes.

"This feels way weird," said Erika. "I don't have pants on!"

"Doing all these buttons made my fingers hurt," said Brandon T. after he figured out how to fasten his new pants.

"Ten buttons to close up a pair of pants is kind of crazy," agreed Max. "The excuse they use is that they didn't have zippers yet."

Once their bonnets were tied and suspenders buttoned,

the kids learned about the manners that went along with their nineteenth-century clothing.

"You all look so different; do you feel any different? Well, I do," said Norma, who had also changed her clothes. "This old-fashioned dress makes me feel more prim and proper. And people did behave differently in the nineteenth century, especially children."

Girls would never do anything so unladylike as run, Norma explained. They would skip instead. And they would never, goodness gracious, sit so their skirts would hike up. Both boys and girls were taught respect for their elders, which included never interrupting or talking back to any adult.

"I'm glad I didn't live back then," Catherine said (but not until later, when she wasn't interrupting anyone).

"When you greet people, say 'good day' or 'hello,'" said Darlene, continuing the lesson. "Girls, you can curtsy if you want to. Boys, you can take off your hats. But don't use the word 'hi,' because it simply didn't exist yet. Does anyone know any other words that weren't used then?"

Dressed and ready, the kids went into the 1800s.

"Cool," shouted Garrett.

"That's right," answered Darlene. "'Cool' described the temperature outside. 'Awesome' described mountains, and you didn't say 'wicked' unless you were talking about someone very mean. Things that you liked were 'splendid' or 'very interesting.'

"At first, you'll make mistakes; it's hard to get used to acting as if you lived in a different time period," Darlene said. "But soon it will begin to feel natural. Then you can really have fun imagining yourself as a person in the eighteen hundreds!"

CHAPTER 3

SOME FAMILY HISTORY

THE KIDS explored the village of Kings Landing together, but they each had their own home base. Kings Landing is filled with nineteenth-century houses that once belonged to real families. Some of these houses show what life was like in the 1820s and '30s, while others represent how people lived in the 1840s and the rest of the century. In the Morehouse house, for example, it is 1820 and

ABOVE: "Can you imagine a grown-up scrunching into this bathtub?" asked Krista.

LEFT: "Sometimes I feel like I'm in a museum," said Amanda.

Mrs. Morehouse cooks over a large open fireplace and gets her water from a well in the yard. By 1840, the Ingrahams have running water inside their home, and in 1860, the Joslins cook dinner on a wood-burning stove.

At night, the kids slept in a more modern house just outside the village. But they spent many daytime hours in the village's homes, visiting their "aunts" and "uncles" (played by museum interpreters). Talking to these "relatives," helping with chores, and sitting down to family dinners was the week's best history lesson.

"Sometimes, when I'm gardening or dusting and no one else is around, I can pretend I'm really from the eighteen hundreds," said Lorena.

"But it would be so different," said Amanda, thinking of life for her Hagerman family. "They didn't have electricity for refrigerators or lights. They didn't even have batteries—so when it was dark, it was really dark."

Looking at a bedroom with a bed, a dresser,

ABOVE: "We try to keep all the food covered," said Aunt Ingraham, "because the flies just love to visit."

LEFT: "Is that ham we're having for dinner?" asked Allison. "Yes," replied Aunt Joslin. "That's one less pig running around outside."

and not much else, Brandon M. realized that people back then didn't have as many things as we do today. "This room is okay," he said, "but my room at home has an alarm clock and books and a CD player and a real closet with a lot of clothes in it."

Comfort is another thing we have a lot more of, too, especially where beds are concerned. Some houses in Kings Landing had beautiful canopy beds with feather mattresses. But others had beds with straw mattresses that felt lumpy and hard.

WHAT IS THIS THING?

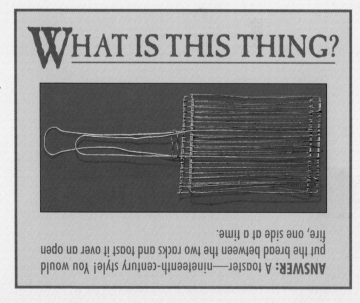

ANSWER: A toaster—nineteenth-century style! You would put the bread between the two racks and toast it over an open fire, one side at a time.

WHAT IS THIS THING?

"I haven't tried out one of those straw mattresses yet, but they look real uncomfortable," said Alex. "You'd have to be pretty tired to like it."

"If you worked all day the way they did, you would be," answered Hilary.

The kids worked a bit themselves. There was plenty of work to do around any nineteenth-century house, even for visiting cousins. "I swept the floor and fetched wood shavings from the cooper's shop to help start the fire in the kitchen stove," said Garrett.

"At home, I set the table and make my bed," said Krista. "I like the chores I do here much better—like baking and taking food out to the pigs."

Amanda helped get dinner ready. "I miss a normal carrot peeler," she said as she scraped vegetables with a knife. Then she started to shuck corn. "Now that I think about it," she added, "I wish someone in the future would invent a corn peeler."

When the kids sat down to eat at noon, corn and carrots were only a

"I don't think I could live without a real bathroom," said Erika. "I have a major phobia about outhouses."

LEFT: "This is a real pain in the neck," said Brandon M., wearing a yoke to carry two buckets of water.

ABOVE: Aunt Hagerman sent Catherine to pull some carrots for dinner.

RIGHT: At more modern houses, kids could use pumps that brought water into the kitchen. Here's Amy at the Morehouse home drawing water from a well.

RIGHT: "They used to have stoves in their rooms to keep them warm—that's cool!" said Brandon M. (But it did take a lot of wood to keep those stoves going.)

"I wish we had more farms now, like they did then," said Garrett.

small part of their meal. One time, for example, the menu included ham, potatoes, green beans, corn, biscuits, and pie for dessert (which was served at the same time as everything else). As Uncle Joslin explained to Allison, they called this meal "dinner," and it was the biggest one of the day. People needed food

"I like the ways they had fun back then," said Krista, "like having tea and meeting to knit and sew."

to fuel all the hard physical work that followed.

"I really like the food," said Stephanie.

"I do, too," said Garrett. "And I like the fact that a lot of it comes from their own gardens."

"But I can't imagine having to make it all instead of buying some from the store," said Allison. "Even the milk is homemade!"

WHAT'S GOING ON

You think you have a hard time getting ready each morning? Imagine getting into a typical outfit from the 1840s. Here are all the things you'd have to put on before grabbing your dress and bonnet . . .

Petticoats were skirts of cotton or silk worn under dresses. They helped keep a woman warm and made her dress look fuller.

3

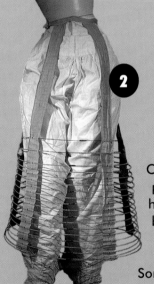

2

Crinolines, petticoats with hoops made out of bone or metal, gave a woman's skirt a full shape. Some crinolines were so big, a woman had a hard time getting through doorways!

1

Pantaloons, worn over drawers (nineteenth-century underpants) protected a woman's legs from cold weather—and from scratchy petticoats.

UNDER THERE?!

4 Corsets, made stiff with bones and laced at the back, made a woman look thinner and more shapely. Sometimes they were laced so tightly, a woman had a hard time breathing. Over time, corsets could even deform the bones in a woman's ribcage.

8 In the 1840s, there was no such thing as a right shoe or a left shoe; both were shaped identically.

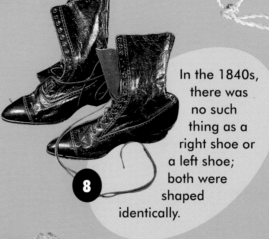

9 In her basket, along with her latest needlework project, our "proper" lady carried a reticule, or handbag . . .

10 . . . which contained her hand-kerchief.

5 The camisole, a type of undershirt, kept a corset from rubbing against a dress.

6 In this era, a pocket was a separate little bag tied around the waist. A woman could put her hand into it through a slit in her skirt.

7 A ribbon or strip of cloth was tied around the top of these cotton stockings to keep them up.

11 A woman wore a day cap indoors and out. This cap protected a woman's hair from dust and the smoke from cooking fires. It also kept her bonnet clean—in those days, a woman only washed her hair about once a month!

CHAPTER 4

SCHOOL DAYS

T HE BELL rang; there should not be another sound," said Norma, patrolling the one-room schoolhouse with a stick in her hand. "Sit up straight in your seats! Put your hands on your desks; it's inspection time! You must come to school clean and tidy!"

Suddenly the kids were quieter than they'd been since their first moments at Kings Landing, when everyone felt new and shy. On that first day, Norma had said she would play the schoolmarm at

"I sort of wish they had invented hooky by now," said Brandon M.

20

Before entering the schoolhouse, the girls had to curtsy and the boys had to bow to the teacher.

ANSWER: This hearse carried coffins to the cemetery. Its runners let it glide over snowy winter roads. In summer, it had wheels instead.

Kings Landing. She had said she'd act like an old-fashioned teacher so the kids could imagine what school was like one hundred and fifty years ago.

After the first session, Amanda had another theory: "The teacher said she'd pretend to be strict, but I think she might really be like that."

"One thing's for sure," said Amy, "if that's what school was like, I wouldn't want to live back then."

One thing *was* for sure—school in the 1800s didn't have classes like music or art or gym. Many small-town schools didn't even have textbooks or other supplies. Teachers sometimes had just one book to use when teaching children how to read. Students learned to write on slates, little blackboards, they could erase and use again. Paper was

In its true light, this transient life regard:
This is a state of trial, not reward.

"Spare the rod, spoil the child" was a very popular expression in the nineteenth century.

so expensive, children only used it to practice penmanship with home-made quill pens.

The kids at Kings Landing also practiced their reading, writing, and arithmetic. They memorized a poem and recited it in class. They lined up and competed in a spelling bee. All the while, Norma watched over them ominously, stick in hand.

"Part of good penmanship is neatness; you must be careful!"

"Time for our mental arithmetic lesson. Forty-eight plus twenty-one—stand to give your answer!"

"Sit up straight, girls. Proper young ladies always have good posture!"

At the end of their last class, Norma said, "Children, erase and put away your slates." When they looked up again, she had an entirely different expression on her face.

WHAT IS THIS THING?

ANSWER: A welcome mat with a little more backbone, this boot scraper was used to remove mud from shoes before people went indoors.

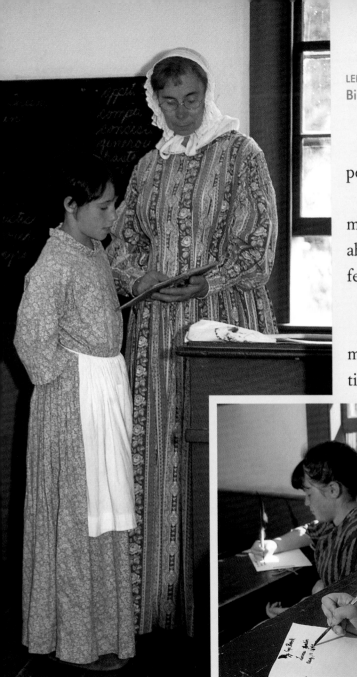

LEFT: Children used to practice reading from books like the Bible or *Aesop's Fables*.

"Wow, she *does* know how to smile," Sam whispered to her neighbor.

"School's over for the week, so I can be my normal self again," said Norma. "And we can talk about how school in the eighteen hundreds was different from the way it is now."

"The teacher was so strict," several kids called out.

"Actually, teachers long ago would have been much stricter than I was," Norma replied. "Sometimes a teacher was just a sixteen-year-old girl teaching boys her age or older. She had to keep control. This stick I'm carrying around wasn't just for pointing, you know. If you misbehaved, it would go down on your knuckles or across your knees."

INSET: Quill pens were made from goose feathers sharpened with penknives and dipped in ink. The Kings Landing kids quickly discovered they were very hard to use without making blobs and blotches.

23

"Our parents wouldn't let you do that," said Max.

"Parents today would not," Norma agreed, "but back then, your parents would have expected me to help teach you manners and turn you into proper ladies and gentlemen."

Holly raised her hand. "This school is so much smaller than mine at home," she said, pointing out another difference.

"That's right, just one room for grades one through six," said Norma. "But children didn't go to school every day. Some missed weeks at a time to help their families. And many of you older ones would already be out working."

"But I'm only thirteen," said Amanda.

"Yes but when you think about it, a lot of the education you needed to live your nineteenth-century life was gotten somewhere else," Norma replied. "Boys, you were apprenticed to your father or uncle to learn a trade. Girls, you would learn to keep house by working with your mothers. Anyway, if you had come to school regularly, year in and year out, it wouldn't take *that* long before you knew as much as the teacher."

The kids thought the idea of children their age knowing as much as a teacher was ridiculous.

"You laugh," said Norma, "but where do you think your teacher learned what she knew?"

"Was there anything you liked better about this school?" Norma added.

"You have to stand when you speak," said Krista. "I like that because everyone pays attention to you."

"It was much quieter," said Robin, "so it was easier to learn the poem we had to memorize."

"The desks are different, but I like them," said Julie.

"These are actual desks from a nineteenth-century schoolhouse," said Norma. "Take a moment to think of all the children who have sat at them, all the history that has happened here.

"Now, class dismissed."

ALL WORK AND NO PLAY ...

A T RECESS, nineteenth-century children used to play games like tag and crack-the-whip. If they needed a ball, they often used an inflated pig's bladder.

"I think some of their games were better," said Amanda. "Now, unless they're playing sports, kids don't have as many games they play outside."

Here are some of the other ways that nineteenth-century children had fun in the days before video games and TV.

Guess who won this game of checkers!

Nineteenth-century children made work fun by having friends join in. In this "wool-picking bee," the kids got wool ready for spinning by picking out the sticks and burrs. "Talk and laugh," said Darlene, "but do a good job. You wouldn't want any twigs in there if your mom was knitting your woolen underwear!"

"Square dancing is sort of fun," said Megan, "but I'd never do it at home."

"Cool," said Alex, after he hit his croquet ball through the wicket. "Oh, it feels a little warm to me," replied Darlene, gently reminding Alex to have a nineteenth-century reaction next time he made a good shot.

27

WOMEN'S WORK

AFTER THEIR stay at Kings Landing, the girls had a new understanding of the expression "A woman's work is never done." In the nineteenth century, most women did not work outside their homes, but taking care of a house and children was work enough. Without electricity or modern appliances, women did all their chores by hand. Imagine first weaving the cloth, then sewing the clothes for an entire family. Imagine preparing three meals a day, when cooking included making every loaf of bread and hunk of cheese. Then there was the cleaning, the washing, the mending . . .

The girls had known before that nineteenth-century women didn't have as many choices and rights. But they didn't like being in that position themselves. "Why can't we go to work at the blacksmith shop or drive the oxen?" asked Erika.

"Well, you're not interested in such things," explained Wendy, trying to tell Erika about the person she would have been in the 1800s.

WHAT IS THIS THING?

ANSWER: This ice-cream scoop has a knob on top that turns the inside blades and releases the ice cream.

Erika wasn't buying it. "Oh yes I am interested," she said. "The nineteenth century wasn't fair."

TENDING THE ANIMALS

Although everyone took care of a farm's animals, jobs like milking cows generally fell to women. Before refrigerators, milk was hard to keep, so women used to turn it into butter and cheese. But first they had to get it out of the cow.

"It's like squeezing one of those stress balls," said Catherine.

"I don't think there's any milk left," said Jillian, even though they had barely begun.

During Stephanie's turn, the cow flicked her tail right into Stephanie's face.

"That's just the cow's way of saying 'good morning,'" said Harry the farmer.

"I don't think so," said Stephanie. "I think she's saying, 'You're not doing it fast enough; let someone else try.'"

As the girls struggled to cover the bottom of their pail with milk, the farmer came out from milking another cow carrying a foamy, steaming pailful.

"Holy cow," said Erika.

"That's the idea," said Catherine.

"This is a little gross," said Amy. "I wouldn't like to be a cow."

"No doubt about it," said Catherine, "they're real pigs!"

29

CHURNING BUTTER

"Not much longer now; it's finally turning into butter," said Aunt Joslin.

The girls were glad they were almost finished; churning butter is hard work. They had pumped the churn's pole up and down until the cream inside bubbled, then foamed, and finally formed nuggets of butter.

Next they poured the mixture into a butter tray, draining off the leftover liquid called buttermilk. After rinsing the lumps with cold water, adding salt for flavor, and working them all together with a paddle, the butter was ready for tasting.

Lorena liked it. "I'd say 'awesome,' but we're not supposed to," she said.

"Not me," said Sam. "Now that I know how real butter is made, I'll never eat it again."

"Don't worry," said Amy, "this is not the same as what you buy in the store."

"I think it's better because we made it ourselves," said Allison.

It takes twenty to forty minutes to churn cream into butter.

If all the buttermilk isn't washed out, the butter spoils very quickly.

"I think I don't like this butter because it comes from the cows we milked," said Amy.

To make yarn, you must comb the wool . . .

SPINNING

When Sarah and Hilary looked at the sheep at Kings Landing, they saw cute, woolly animals. Girls in the nineteenth century also would have seen woven cloth for dresses and yarn to be knitted into socks and long underwear. But turning wool into clothing is a long process.

After the wool is cleaned, it must be pulled and stretched into a soft, white cloud. Then it is brushed on a tool called a card, and rolled off into a cylinder that looks like a lamb's tail. Nineteenth-century women took these rolls to their spinning wheels to twist them into yarn for knitting or weaving. But spinning wheels are hard to master. So when girls first started learning to make yarn, they began with a drop spindle instead.

Darlene showed the girls at Kings Landing how to draw out the wool fibers and twist them into smooth, strong thread by turning the drop spindle. "Don't get frustrated," she said. "It takes a while to learn."

"Mine would have turned out as good if I had just rolled the wool between my hands," said Erika.

. . . and practice, practice, practice on your spindle!

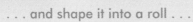

. . . and shape it into a roll . . .

LAUNDRY

"Girls, we're doing the Hagermans' laundry," announced a counselor named Sharlene. "Luckily they live in 1870 and are very modern. They have a washing machine."

The Hagermans' washing machine hardly fit in with the girls' idea of modern. They had to do the wash, rinse, and spin cycles themselves. The girls wet the clothes, then sudsed them up with soap made of beef fat and lye. Then they rocked the top of the machine back and forth to clean and rinse the clothes.

"This seems like a lot of work," said Amanda.

"Yes, but they washed less laundry than we do," Sharlene explained. "Most people could only afford one outfit besides their Sunday best. Luckily they also had different standards of hygiene."

"One outfit each week wouldn't be so bad," said Julie. "At least you wouldn't have to think about what to put on in the morning."

ABOVE: Laundry day, typically the first day of the week, was called "Blue Monday." The girls thought that was because no one liked doing the wash, but it was actually because people used bluing, a liquid that made white clothes whiter.

LEFT: Women usually tucked underwear under bigger items so it couldn't be seen on the clothesline.

BAKING

Baking in the 1800s meant no electric mixers or microwaves, not even a cake mix. In fact, in the early part of the century, cooks only had whole wheat flour to stir into their cookies and pies.

"We are lucky. It's 1870 in our house," said Aunt Perley while teaching the girls how to make crumb cake. "So we have baking powder and the lovely white flour that makes such a difference in baking."

As Sam and Stephanie measured and stirred, Aunt Perley explained that most women in the 1800s made their own bread, biscuits, and desserts. Then she showed the girls a nineteenth-century oven thermometer: She put her hand inside the oven. Since she was able to keep it there until she counted to ten, the oven was hot enough to bake, but not hot enough to burn.

"It *is* hot in here," said Sam as she put their cake in the oven.

"That's why ladies always have pink cheeks," said Aunt Perley.

BELOW: Sam's peek-a-boo oven, with doors on either side, lets her see if her cake is cooking evenly.

LEFT: Waiting for the cake to come out of the oven, Stephanie had her first cup of tea brewed from loose tea leaves instead of a tea bag.

Sampler text:
ABCDEFGHIJKL MNOPQRST
UVWXYZ. 123456789
abcdefghijklmnopqrstuvwxyz
ABCDEFGHIJKLeM
NOPQRSTVVW
XYZ. Suffer little children to come unto
me and forbid them not
Elizabeth J Valentine aged 8

NEEDLEWORK

In the nineteenth century, needlework was considered a more important skill for women than reading or math. Women spent hours mending old clothes, sewing new ones, and making things like patchwork quilts for their homes. They usually took a small project with them on visits to friends so they could talk *and* work on an embroidered pincushion or handkerchief.

At their sewing bee, the girls made a reticule, a small nineteenth-century version of a purse. Krista was glad. "I'm getting a cold," she said. "I can put Kleenex in it."

"They didn't have Kleenex back then," said Holly.

ABOVE: Making samplers, girls practiced different sewing stitches and learned their letters and numbers at the same time.

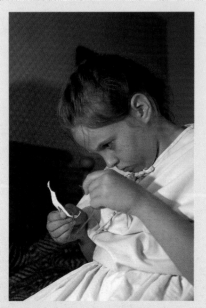

LEFT: "I bet I'm going to sew my purse to my dress," said Hilary.

"That's why I'm hiding it in the bag," Krista replied.

Back in the 1800s, girls learned to sew as early as age four. Many of the girls at Kings Landing had never really used a needle and thread before. Being older didn't make their lesson any easier.

"I'm always pricking myself," said Krista.

"Look on the bright side," said Sarah, "burning yourself on the stove is worse."

WHAT IS THIS THING?

ANSWER: No, it's not a paddle for removing pizzas from the oven. This paddle was used to beat and fluff up straw and feather mattresses.

CHAPTER 6

WHAT IS THIS THING?

ANSWER: Through the ages, people have warmed up their cold bed sheets with a hot-water bottle. In the twentieth century, these contraptions have been made of rubber. One hundred years before, they used pottery.

MEN'S WORK

IN THE nineteenth century, a boy often couldn't choose the work he'd do as a grown-up. He usually took on the job his father had, whether it was farming or printing or boot making. When a boy became an apprentice to another tradesman, however, he would often live and work with his new master. It was like attending blacksmithing or barrel-making school, but with only one teacher. Over the years, the apprentice worked for the tradesman, learning more and more, until he knew enough to become a master craftsman himself.

The boys at Kings Landing didn't like the idea of not being able to choose their own future. But they did like the different kinds of work that men did in the 1800s.

"Be careful," said Mark as Max picked up the potatoes Brandon T. unearthed with his hoe. "We don't want any fingers mixed in with our spuds."

FARMING

When the farmer discovered Brandon T. had never worked in his garden at home, he was surprised. "What do you do when you're not in school?" Harry asked.

"Play video games," answered Brandon.

"When I was your age," replied Harry, "I was milking cows morning and night."

In the nineteenth century, farming was more a way of life than a business. Farmers grew enough crops to feed their family and animals. They raised sheep to have wool for clothes and kept cows for milk, cheese, and butter. Any surplus—extra apples or cheese, for example—would be traded or sold to buy supplies at the general store.

It was harvesttime when the boys were at Kings Landing. After they dug up potatoes and picked cucumbers, they used a sickle to harvest corn stalks. Harry explained that they fed these corn stalks and turnips to the cows.

"I hate turnips," replied Max. "That's what I would do if I grew 'em."

Farmers used every part of the corn plant. Corn was ground into cornmeal; the stalks were fed to cattle; and the leftover cobs were turned into pipes and dolls, even nineteenth-century toilet paper!

"I like this," said Alex. "I could grow up to be a farmer."

OXEN

"Having a good team of oxen was the nineteenth-century version of macho, like having a fancy car today," said Gene, the oxen trainer. "A farmer was proud of owning a set matched in color and weight."

Unlike a car, you can't take a team of oxen for a quick spin around the block; oxen don't do anything quickly. But they were a great help to nineteenth-century farmers. Oxen could carry much heavier loads than horses. They could haul three times their own weight—and they weighed in at more than a ton each! Unlike horses, oxen were controlled by voice commands, not by reins. So a farmer had his hands free to steer his plow and other machinery.

"Time to get 'em on the road," said Gene. "Say 'haw' to make them go left, and say 'gee' for right."

At first, when the boys "geed" and "hawed," the oxen stayed right where they were.

"Come on, boys," said Gene. "Say 'haw' in the same way your dad might send you to your room. They respond to a firm tone of voice."

Finally, the oxen started plodding their way to the woodpile.

"Are they friendly?" asked Alex when it was his turn to drive.

"Sort of," answered Gene, "but I wouldn't want a twenty-three-hundred-pound beast to show me too much affection."

LEFT: A boy asked if the caps on the oxen's horns kept them from poking people. "They are just for decoration," answered Gene. "If he wanted to poke you with them on, he'd just make a larger hole."

SAWMILL

"Want to power up the sawmill?" asked Brad, the miller. As Brandon T. pulled the lever, water gushed onto the waterwheel. The giant wheel slowly started to turn, then picked up speed. This motion created the power that ran the saw and the winch that hauled the logs into the mill.

"Thank goodness for water power and pulleys," Brad said as he showed the boys how to move the logs up the ramp into the mill. "These logs are well over fifteen hundred pounds apiece. Imagine trying to get one of these big fellas in all by yourself."

As the boys watched the saw cut the log, Brad explained more about working in an 1830s sawmill. "Since we use water power, we can only work when the river isn't frozen, from April to December. Then we work sunrise to sunset—in June, that's sixteen hours a day.

"Now I'll show you how much money we got paid," he said, pulling some coins from his pocket. "Just four shillings a day."

The boys stared at the coins in his hand.

"It wasn't much," Brad agreed, "but remember, it was worth a lot more then."

ABOVE RIGHT: Max used a pike pole to pull a floating log to the sawmill.

RIGHT: Logs came into the mill using a system of ropes and pulleys. "It's like playing tug-of-war against a machine," said Max.

BLACKSMITH

"Come right in, boys," said the blacksmith. "I could use a few apprentices."

No surprise, a blacksmith usually had one of the busiest shops in any country town. The blacksmith made the tools men used on the farm and women used in the kitchen. He made shoes for the oxen; he even made the hinges for their barn doors.

A blacksmith's apprentice started learning the trade by making something much easier: a nail. Eventually an apprentice could make one nail every seven seconds, but the boys only had a chance to try once. They carefully heated a rod of iron in the forge and pounded the end on an anvil. Heat, pound, heat, pound, until the nail was done.

"Ouch! I didn't think it would still be hot!" said Alex, inspecting the red dot on his finger.

RIGHT: Garrett pumped air on the fire to make it burn hotter, which helped heat this metal rod.

"Oh yes," said the blacksmith, "even when it's black, iron's temperature can still be eight hundred degrees."

"I'd be a blacksmith," said Brandon M., at the end of his turn. "I think it's fun."

"The only problem," the blacksmith answered, "is that blacksmiths often went deaf because of that constant loud sound of metal hitting metal."

"Are you deaf?" asked Garrett.

"What did you say?" the blacksmith jokingly replied.

"Garrett," the blacksmith said, "you are doing a bang-up job!"

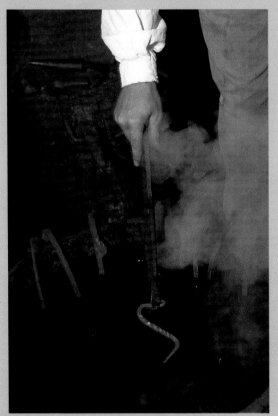

Blacksmiths often cooled hot metal by dipping it in water. "Look at that steam," said Alex. "That's how hot it was when I burned my finger."

THE PRINT SHOP

"Today we just punch letters on a keyboard and computers take care of the rest," said the printer in Kings Landing's print shop. "In 1890, printing was a much harder process."

Whether making a poster or a whole newspaper, a nineteenth-century printer had to construct a page, one letter at a time. After he spelled out each word, letter by letter, he put it in a flat tray. Once the

INSET: When Alex pumped a foot treadle, the press moved the type forward so it "pressed" onto the paper and printed his poster.

LEFT: Small print shops made everything from advertising fliers and stationery to tickets for special events.

When type is set, it is always upside down and backward. Can you read what this says?

Letters in a type case were not arranged alphabetically. The ones used most often were put in the easiest places to reach.

whole page of type was finished and locked into place, it went into the press to be inked and printed.

The boys didn't think it was too hard to find the type to make the "Wanted" posters they took home as souvenirs. But imagine picking out all the letters in a newspaper page without making mistakes.

Alex's reaction? "If I didn't have a computer," he said, "I think I'd rather write out my homework than do it this way."

CHAPTER 7

BACK TO THE FUTURE

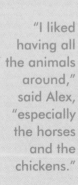

"I liked having all the animals around," said Alex, "especially the horses and the chickens."

O N THEIR last night at Kings Landing, the kids started getting a little homesick for the twentieth century.

"I can't wait to go home and kill some aliens on my computer," said Garrett.

"Once I get my normal clothes on again, I'm not going to take them off," said Sam. "I think I'm gonna sleep in them my first night home."

"On *my* first night," said Lorena, "whatever else I do, I'm going to watch *The Simpsons.*"

As the girls changed into their nineteenth-century sleepwear, they all agreed that the nightcaps should stay in the 1800s where they belonged. But many were glad they could take their nightgowns home with them. And they wished they could take other parts of the nineteenth century home as well.

"I liked milking the cow," said Robin.

"I liked the fact that kids could go around the town all by themselves," said Krista. "Everybody knew everybody, so you didn't have to worry."

"I liked being able to walk to school instead of taking a long bus ride," said Amanda. "That way you could meet up with other kids and talk."

"I liked the quiet," said Allison. "No car horns or sirens, no jackhammers."

But the kids also found their visit to the past gave them a fresh look at their lives in the present. Suddenly they valued parts of the twentieth century they had taken for granted because they had never known life without them.

WHAT IS THIS THING?

ANSWER: An eggbeater!

Many girls liked their nineteenth-century nightgowns, but when Brandon T. found out the kids could take their night-clothes home, he said, "I don't think I'll ever wear mine again."

45

WHAT IS THIS THING?

ANSWER: Outhouses seem pretty far off when you need them in the middle of the night. In the days before plumbing, this was the closest thing they had to an indoor toilet. Notice the lid on the chair seat opens to a pot below.

First and foremost—phones, electricity, cars, the technology that affects every part of modern life.

"I'm sort of a TV fanatic and I've really missed it," said Garrett. "That and my remote-control car."

"After walking on rocks in these shoes all week, I really miss good roads," said Amanda.

"One thing I like a lot less here is the bugs," said Hilary.

"Wait a minute," said Catherine, "We have the same bugs now, too."

"Yeah," Hilary answered, "but they didn't have anything to kill them with back then."

"The thing that surprised and bothered me most was that you weren't supposed to run," said Sarah.

"That's right," agreed Allison, who started thinking about all the rules the nineteenth century had for girls. "At home, I'm used to acting normal instead of being so very, very, very polite."

"I can't imagine living in a time when women couldn't vote," said Catherine. "It would make me so mad."

"I don't like the fact that Kings Landing has a river the boys would be able to swim in back then—but not me," said Erika. "And I don't like that the guys got to do a lot of things we couldn't do."

"I'd like to be a blacksmith," said Hilary, "but I like sewing, too."

"That's right," said Amy, "I'd like to stay being a girl, but I'd like to do boy things."

The next day, the kids had their last lunch of chicken raised on the farm, vegetables they'd picked from the garden, and biscuits baked in a woodstove served with butter they had churned themselves. Then they met up with their parents and their twentieth-century lives. Bonnets were untied for the last time; hair was unbraided. Suspenders were yanked off shoulders and pants with buttons replaced by zippered blue jeans.

One by one, the kids left Kings Landing with their families. A bunch of them immediately turned their car radios to local rock stations. Amanda dug into the first bag of chips she'd had all week. Julie and Holly headed for a nearby restaurant that served burgers and fries. Despite this leap into the twentieth century, many kids realized they were taking part of the past home with them.

"I had tried doing needlework before, but thought it was too hard," said Lorena. "I'm going to start doing embroidery again."

"When I was at Kings Landing, it was like I was a different girl," said Amanda. "People were friendly back then. When we walked through the village, they would say 'hello' to everybody they passed. I'm going to remember that when I go home."

"I know what's gonna happen once we go home," said Allison. "Instead of saying 'That's cool,' we'll say, 'Isn't that splendid!' and everyone will look at us as if we are weird!"

Back to the twentieth century.

47

GLOSSARY

ANVIL—a block of iron on which metal is shaped by hammering

APPRENTICE—someone who is learning a trade

CARD—a wire-toothed brush used to untangle wool before spinning

CHURN—to stir or shake cream to make butter

COOPER—someone who makes or repairs wooden barrels

CURTSY—a way women show respect by bending their knees and lowering their body with one foot dropped behind them

DROP SPINDLE—a wooden tool used to spin fiber into thread

FORGE—a hearth where metals are heated in a blacksmith's shop

HEARSE—a vehicle that transports coffins

HOOKY—slang for being out of school without permission

HYGIENE—the science that deals with being healthy

INTERPRETER—someone who works at a museum explaining history to visitors

MACHO—having an exaggerated sense of maleness

PENMANSHIP—the skill of good handwriting

PHOBIA—a strong fear of something

PIKE POLE—a stick with a metal spike on one end

POSTURE—a way of holding one's body

PULLEY—a simple machine where a rope placed over a wheel allows someone to lift a heavy load easily

QUILL—a pen made out of a feather

RETICULE—a woman's drawstring purse

SCHOOLMARM—a teacher

SHUCK—to peel the husk off an ear of corn

SICKLE—a tool with a semicircular blade used to cut grain or grass

SLATE—a piece of a stone that is used to write on

SPINNING WHEEL—a wooden machine with a wheel used to spin thread or yarn

SPUDS—slang word for potatoes

TREADLE—a pedal that helps power a machine

TYPE—a small block of metal with a letter on it that works like a stamp when inked and pressed on paper

WINCH—a machine that helps lift heavy loads

FURTHER READING

Other Nonfiction Books about Life in the 1800s

Costabel, Eva Deutsch. *A New England Village*. New York: Atheneum, 1983.

Greenwood, Barbara. *A Pioneer Sampler: The Daily Life of a Pioneer Family in 1840*. New York: Ticknor and Fields Books for Young Readers, 1995.

Fiction about Life in the 1800s

Lawlor, Laurie. *Addie Across the Prairie*. Minstrel Books, 1991.

Turner, Ann. *Grasshopper Summer*. New Jersey: A Troll Book, 1991.

Wilder, Laura Ingalls. *The Little House Books* (series). New York: HarperCollins, various dates.

Fiction about Time Travel

Bond, Nancy. *Another Shore*. New York: McElderry Books, 1988.

Haddix, Margaret Peterson. *Running Out of Time*. New York: Aladdin, 1997.

Scieszka, Jon. *The Time Warp Trio* (series). New York: Puffin, various dates.

Yolen, Jane. *The Devil's Arithmetic*. New York: Puffin, 1990.

For more information about the Visiting Cousins Program at Kings Landing, contact:

Education Office
Kings Landing Historical Settlement
20 Kings Landing Service Road
Prince William, NB
Canada E6K 3W3
Telephone: 506-363-4999
E-mail: kings.landing@gov.nb.ca
www.gov.nb.ca/kingslanding

j1973.5   Goodman, Susan E.
GOO
           Ultimate field trip
           4.

$17.00

DATE			